In memory of Rev. Stanley T. Nakowicz, October 5, 1941 - December 3, 2012.
Thank you for all your kindness, support, and enthusiasm
throughout the creation of this book.

- Mark Perry

Thank you to my mom and dad.
My education and support were the best gifts.

- Lia Marcoux

Produced and Published by Delor Francis Press
873 Atwells Avenue
Providence, Rhode Island 02909
www.delorfrancis.com

Graphic Design by WOMA Design, Newport, Rhode Island
www.womadesign.com

Library of Congress Cataloging-in-Publication data:
Perry, Mark, 1974-
"Post" Mark : Santa's misfit postman / written by
Mark Perry ; illustrated by Lia Marcoux. -- 1st ed.
 p. cm.
SUMMARY: A young boy, Mark, is called a misfit
because he dreams of travel and writing stories about
his adventures. Despite his classmates' taunts, Mark
finds a place to fit in with Santa's elves and becomes
"Post" Mark, the North Pole postman.
Audience: Ages 3-8.
LCCN 2012956576
ISBN 978-0-9838947-0-4

1. Outcasts--Juvenile fiction. 2. Elves--Juvenile
fiction. 3. Letter carriers--Juvenile fiction.
[1. Outcasts--Fiction. 2. Elves--Fiction. 3. Letter
carriers--Fiction.] I. Marcoux, Lia, ill. II. Title.

PZ7.P43535Pos 2013   [E]
QBI13-600009

First Edition

'Post' Mark – Santa's Misfit Postman

Written by Mark Perry   Illustrated by Lia Marcoux

DF

Delor Francis
PRESS

On the school playground, Mark always felt like a misfit.

His knees would **wobble** and his legs would **shake**,
and Mark worried the kids would laugh at him.

Mark's classmates didn't understand him because he liked daydreaming and writing stories about faraway places more than he liked hide-and-go-seek, tag, and dodgeball.

The kids laughed at him and said,
"You can't fly around the world.
You'll never go **anywhere**
or see **anything**!"

Mark was hurt by his classmates' taunts.

He didn't fit in, but he never let that stop him
from writing stories and dreaming dreams.

Mark dreamed those dreams all the way to university
where he met lots of friends who loved to write too.
Finally, Mark **fit in**!

And, like the dreams he had on the playground,
Mark began traveling all over the world
and writing stories about his adventures.

In the United States, he saw the Statue of Liberty.
It was a birthday gift from France.
Wow! A birthday gift that is 15 stories tall!

In China,

Mark climbed the mountains to tell the world
all about the *giant panda* munching bamboo.

7

In London, he saw the first public zoo in the world!
It opened back in 1829.

In Australia,

he saw a koala bear
and a kangaroo.

Mark's big dreams really had come true!

At the South Pole, Mark met real emperor penguins.
They don't mind living in Antarctica where it's usually
40 degrees below zero.
That's even **colder** than the North Pole!

And yes, Mark went to the North Pole too,
and he did just what you would do at the North Pole ...
he searched for Santa!

But Santa didn't look too jolly the day Mark found him.
"Oh my goodness, Santa, what's wrong?
I thought you were always full of good cheer."

Santa said,

"Well... Look in this room over here."

13

"Wow! Look at all these letters!" Mark said.
"There must be **thousands**!"

"That's the problem," Santa said with a tear in his eye.
"I am so busy getting my sleigh ready,
looking after the reindeer,
and making sure the elves make enough toys
that I can't write to all the girls and boys."

"I sure wish I had an elf
that could help me with my mail,"
Santa said.

"Can't one of your workshop elves help?" Mark asked.

15

"Elves are clever writers,
but they wouldn't be able to deliver the letters.
They've never left the North Pole, and I really need an elf
who knows how to **travel the world**," Santa said.

"I'm not an elf,
but I love to travel the world, Santa.
I've been to **all seven continents**," Mark said.

"Wait! I've got it!" Santa said.

"**You** can deliver my mail! Oh, would you please?"

"I could and I would,

but there's one small problem," Mark said.

"When I was a kid, all the other kids thought I was a misfit."

"A misfit," Santa said.

"How so?"

"Well, writing stories has always been my favorite thing to do, and when I was growing up
all the other kids laughed at me and called me names.
They said I would never go anywhere."

"Ho, ho, ho, Mark!" laughed Santa.

"Now you listen to me.
I have an elf who wants to be a dentist
and a reindeer with a red nose.
To say you're a misfit around here is nonsense."

"I know you are a very good writer and world traveler.
I need someone who can travel all over the world to collect and
deliver the letters with a genuine stamp cancellation, or **'postmark'**
from the North Pole."

"Wow! Did you hear what I just said?

Postmark!

Your name tells me you're the perfect fit – not a misfit at all.

Is it okay if I call you 'Post' Mark?"

"Sure, Santa," Mark said.

"What exactly are you trying to say?"

24

"I'm saying that your visit with me today
is a **Christmas miracle**, 'Post' Mark.
Because you can travel many miles, would you be my postman
and deliver a miracle and a smile to every child?"

"It would be more than an honor, Santa!"

"**Ho, ho, hooray!**" Santa said.

And just like Santa's famous red-nosed reindeer,

'Post' Mark will go down in hi-sto-reeee!

27

Visit 'Post' Mark's website
www.northpolepostman.com
for more fun, games, and activities!

Kids can send their "wish list" to 'Post' Mark,

and he will forward it to Santa!

Be sure to ask your parents' permission beforehand.

Parents can write to 'Post' Mark

and inform Santa of how their children are *really* behaving.

Now there is more reason to be good for goodness sake!

The Place for Kids and Grown-Ups to Communicate with Santa Claus

NORTH POLE
POSTMAN

A Miracle and a Smile for Every Child